The Berenstain Bears® and the SPOOKY SHADOWS

Stan & Jan Berenstain

Reader's Digest
YOUNG FAMILIES
Westport, Connecticut

When Sister Bear was very little, she was afraid of many things.

She was afraid of bugs.

She was afraid of birds.

She was afraid of big dogs.

She was afraid of thunder and lightning.

But the thing she was *most* afraid of was *spooky shadows*.

When Sister got bigger, she was no longer afraid of bugs, birds, and big dogs.

She wasn't even afraid of
thunder and lightning.

But she was still afraid of *spooky shadows.*

"Why are you afraid of spooky shadows?" asked Mama Bear. "Shadows are nothing to be afraid of."

"I don't know," said Sister. "I just am."

"Your mama's right," said Papa Bear. "A shadow is just a shadow. Why are you afraid of them?"

"Because they're so spooky," she said.

Brother Bear thought Sister was silly to be afraid of shadows. He teased her about it.

"Scaredy bear! Scaredy bear! Afraid of your own shadow!" he teased. It wasn't very nice. But sometimes big brothers aren't very nice to little sisters—even big brothers as nice as Brother Bear.

"That's not very nice," said Mama,
"—calling your sister scaredy bear."
"That's right," said Papa. "Besides,
Sister is very brave about most things."

She wasn't afraid of frogs and toads.

She wasn't afraid of spooky-shaped trees.

And one day when a big
spider came and sat down
beside her...

she scared the *spider* away.

But when it got late, and shadows got bigger and longer, Sister got scared.

"Help!" she cried. "SPOOKY SHADOWS!"

She ran up the steps into the tree
house and into Papa's arms.

"We must do something about Sister Bear and spooky shadows," said Mama. "I have an idea," said Papa.

"Look, Sister," he said. "Shadows can be fun." He gave her a flashlight to shine on the wall. Then he made a funny shadow with his hands. It looked like a bird.

Sister looked at Papa's hands. She looked at the shadow on the wall.

"A bird!" she said. Papa wiggled his hands and the bird flapped its wings.

"Oh, goody! It's flapping its wings!"
she said. "May I do it?"

Papa held the flashlight and showed
Sister how to hold her hands.

"Oh, this is fun!" said Sister.

Then Papa showed her how to make a shadow rabbit,

a shadow goose,

and a shadow dog.

Later that night, when they were going up to bed, Sister played a trick on Brother. She made a big shadow bird and flapped its wings.

"Yipe!" he cried. "A spooky shadow!"

"Scaredy bear! Scaredy bear!" she teased. "Scared of a silly shadow bird!"

Then, when they were both
in bed, Sister teased Brother
some more.

She made a rabbit,
a goose, and a dog.
    "Spooky shadows!
Spooky shadows!"
cried Brother.

Papa came. "Stop teasing your brother with those shadows, Sister," he said with a smile. "I guess you're not afraid of spooky shadows anymore."

"I guess not," she said.

But Brother was—just a little.